398.21
Gag
c.2

duplicate card 68255
6-5-81

Gags, Wanda

The Sorcerer's Apprentice

398.21
Gag
c.2

68255

Gags, Wanda

The Sorcerer's Apprentice

Siskiyou County Schools Library
Yreka, California

THE SORCERER'S APPRENTICE

illustrated by
Margot Tomes

Coward, McCann & Geoghegan, Inc.
New York

Wanda Gág's
THE SORCERER'S APPRENTICE

LIBRARY OF CONGRESS CATALOGING IN PUBLICATION DATA

Gág, Wanda, 1893–1946.   The sorcerer's apprentice.

The text was adapted by W. Gág from several sources,
and originally appeared in the collection More Tales
from Grimm.

SUMMARY: A sorcerer's apprentice learns his master's
spells on the sly and finds they come in handy when
he is in danger.

    [1. Fairy tales. 2. Folklore]   I. Tomes, Margot.
II. Title

PZ8.G123So   398.2'1'0943   78-23990   ISBN 0-698-20481-6

Typography by Diane Zuromskis
Printed in the United States of America

For Ferd

A man found himself in need of a helper for his workshop, and one day as he was walking along the outskirts of a little hamlet he met a boy with a bundle slung over his shoulder. Stopping him, the man said, "Good morning, my lad. I am looking for an apprentice. Have you a master?"

"No," said the boy. "I have just this morning said good-bye to my mother and am now off to find myself a trade."

"Good," said the man. "You look as though you might be just the lad I need. But wait, do you know anything about reading and writing?"

"Oh yes!" said the boy.

"Too bad!" said the man. "You won't do after all. I have no use for anyone who can read and write."

"Pardon me?" said the boy. "If it was *reading* and *writing* you were talking about, I misunderstood you. I thought you asked if I knew anything about *eating* and *fighting*— those two things I am able to do well, but as to reading and writing, that is something I know nothing about."

"Well!" cried the man. "Then you are just the fellow I want. Come with me to my workshop, and I will show you what to do."

The boy, however, had had his wits about him. He could read and write well enough and had only pretended to be a fool. Wondering why a man should prefer to have an unschooled helper, he thought to himself, "I smell a rat. There is something strange about this, and I had better keep my eyes and ears open."

While he was pondering over this, his new master was leading him into the heart of a deep forest. Here in a small clearing stood a house and, as soon as they entered it, the boy could see that this was no ordinary workshop.

At one end of a big room was a huge hearth with a copper cauldron hanging in it; at the other end was a small alcove lined with many big books. A mortar and pestle stood on a bench; bottles and sieves, measuring scales and oddly shaped glassware were strewn about on the table.

Well! It did not take the clever young apprentice very long to realize that he was working for a magician or sorcerer of some kind and so, although he pretended to be quite stupid, he kept his eyes and ears open, and tried to learn all he could.

"Sorcery—that is a trade I would dearly love to master!" said the boy to himself. "A mouthful of good chants and charms would never come amiss to a poor fellow like me, and with them I might even be able to do some good in the world."

There were many things the boy had to do. Sometimes he was ordered to stir the evil-smelling broths which bubbled in the big copper cauldron. At other times he had to grind up herbs and berries—and other things too gruesome to mention—in the big mortar and pestle.

It was also his task to sweep up the workshop, to keep the fire burning in the big hearth, and to gather the strange materials needed by the man for the broths and brews he was always mixing.

This went on day after day, week after week, and month after month, until the boy was almost beside himself with curiosity. He

was most curious about the thick, heavy
books in the alcove. How often he had won-
dered about them, and how many times had
he been tempted to take a peep between
their covers!

But, remembering that he was not sup-
posed to know how to read or write, he had
been wise enough never to show the least
interest in them. At last there came a day
when he made up his mind to see what was
in them, no matter what the risk.

"I'll try it before another day dawns," he
thought.

That night he waited until the sorcerer was sound asleep and was snoring loudly in his bedchamber. Then, creeping out of his straw couch, the boy took a light into the corner of the alcove and began paging through one of the heavy volumes. What was written in them has never been told, but they were conjuring books, each and every one of them.

And from that time on, the boy read in them silently, secretly, for an hour or two, night after night. In this way he learned many magic tricks: chants and charms and countercharms; recipes for philters and potions, for broths and brews and witches' stews; signs mystic and cabalistic, and other helpful spells of many kinds.

All these he memorized carefully, and it was not long before he sometimes was able to figure out what kind of charms his master was working, what brand of potion he was mixing, what sort of stews he was brewing.

And what kind of charms and potions and stews were they? Alas, they were all wicked ones! Now the boy knew that he was not working for an ordinary magician, but for a cruel, dangerous sorcerer.

And because of this, the boy made a plan, a bold one.

He went on with his nightly studies until his head was swarming with magic recipes and incantations. He even had time to work at them in the daytime, for the sorcerer sometimes left the workshop for hours—working harm and havoc on mortals, no doubt. At such times the boy would try out a few bits of his newly learned wisdom.

He began with simple things, such as changing the cat into a bee

and back to cat again,

making a viper out of the poker,

an imp out of the broom, and so on. Sometimes he was successful, often he was not.
So he said to himself, "The time is not yet
ripe."

One day, after the sorcerer had again gone forth on one of his mysterious trips, the boy hurried through his work, and had just settled himself in the dingy alcove with one of the conjuring books on his knees, when the master returned unexpectedly. The boy, thinking fast, pointed smilingly at one of the pictures, after which he quietly closed the book and went on with his work as though nothing were amiss.

But the sorcerer was not deceived.

"If the wretch can read," he thought, "he may learn how to outwit me. And I can't send him off with a beating and a 'bad speed to you,' either—doubtless he knows too much already and will reveal all my fine mean tricks, and then I can't have any more sport working mischief on man and beast."

He acted quickly.

With one leap he rushed at the boy, who in turn made a spring for the door.

"Stop!" cried the sorcerer. "You shall not escape me!"

He was about to grab the boy by the collar when the quick-witted lad mumbled a powerful incantation by which he changed himself into a bird—and—*Wootsch!*—he had flown into the woods.

The sorcerer, not to be outdone, shouted a charm, thus changing himself into a larger bird—and *Whoosh!*—he was after the little one.

With a new incantation the boy made himself into a fish—and *Whish!*—he was swimming across a big pond.

But the master was equal to this, for, with a few words he made himself into a fish too, a big one, and swam after the little one.

At this the boy changed himself into a still bigger fish,

but the magician, by a master stroke, turned himself into a tiny kernel of grain and rolled into a small crack in a stone where the fish couldn't touch him.

Quickly the boy changed himself into a rooster, and—*Peck! Peck! Peck!*—with his sharp beak he snapped at the kernel of grain and ate it up.

That was the end of the wicked sorcerer, and the boy became the owner of the magic workshop. And wasn't it fine that all the powers and ingredients which had been used for evil by the sorcerer were now in the hands of a boy who would use them only for the good of man and beast?